LIBRARY'S MOST
WANTED

Carolyn Leiloglou   Illustrated by Sarah Pogue

PELICAN PUBLISHING
NEW ORLEANS 2020

Library of Congress Cataloging-in-Publication Data

Names: Leiloglou, Carolyn, author. | Pogue, Sarah, illustrator.
Title: Library's most wanted / Carolyn Leiloglou ; illustrated by Sarah Pogue.
Description: New Orleans, LA : Pelican Publishing, 2020. | Audience: Ages 3-8. | Audience: Grades K-1. | Summary: As "deputy librarian" to her Aunt Nora, Libby is so serious about protecting books that she chases away other book lovers, until she sees that a librarian's real job is to connect books with readers.
Identifiers: LCCN 2019046607 | ISBN 9781455625178 (hardcover) | ISBN 9781455625185 (ebook)
Subjects: CYAC: Libraries—Fiction. | Books and reading—Fiction. | Cowgirls—Fiction.
Classification: LCC PZ7.1.L4558 Lib 2020 | DDC [E]—dc23
LC record available at https://lccn.loc.gov/2019046607

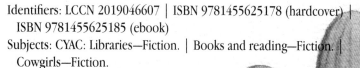

Printed in Malaysia
Published by Pelican Publishing
New Orleans, LA
www.pelicanpub.com

To Arden—love books . . . love people more

When Aunt Nora asked her
to be deputy librarian, Libby
took her job *very* seriously.

She stink-eyed a boy returning a
dog-eared novel.
    She pried a board book from the
clutches of a gnawing toddler.

And when she discovered
the remains of the Wild West
book display . . .

"Yikes! It looks like a twister struck. These books need protecting. And by gum, I'm deputy 'round here."

While Aunt Nora corralled the kids for
story time, Libby hatched her scheme.

Libby was a quick draw. Fast as a rattler,
she sketched a stack of Wanted posters.

The kids gathered 'round.

"Is that a picture of me spilling juice on books?" asked José.

The Juicebox Bandit

"I don't draw on *every* page," said Zoey.

The Crayon Kid

"It's not my fault my dog chewed up a book," said Bryan.

Wild Dog Desperado

"It's my duty to keep these books safe," Libby told them. "Cross me and I'll lasso you to a beanbag chair. Now, skedaddle."

"We're not welcome here," said Sasha. "Let's go."

The kids stampeded to the playground.

Libby surveyed the abandoned children's
section with satisfaction.
She patrolled the aisles.
She rounded up stray books.
She even doodled a few mustaches on her
Wanted posters.

Wild Dog Desperado

The Crayon Kid

The Juicebox Bandit

Finally, she sat down to read. But the children's section was quiet. It was too quiet—quieter than a ghost town.

Libby hightailed it to the circulation counter.

"The library feels so empty today," said Aunt Nora.

"Yup. I reckon the books are safe now," said Libby.

Aunt Nora raised an eyebrow. "Safe from what?"

"From being vandalized by those outlaws."

"Excuse me," said a woman.
"I'm sorry, but I'm afraid my
Sammy loved this book a little too much."
Tarnation! thought Libby. *Another one
bites the dust.*
"Let's take a look," said Aunt Nora. "Libby, why
don't you help Sammy find a new book?"
Libby's eyes bulged. *I have to give this bandit a
chance to ruin another book?* she thought.

Libby sighed. "C'mon." She sulked all the way to the children's section, with Sammy in tow.

"How about a puzzle instead?"
Sammy shook his head.

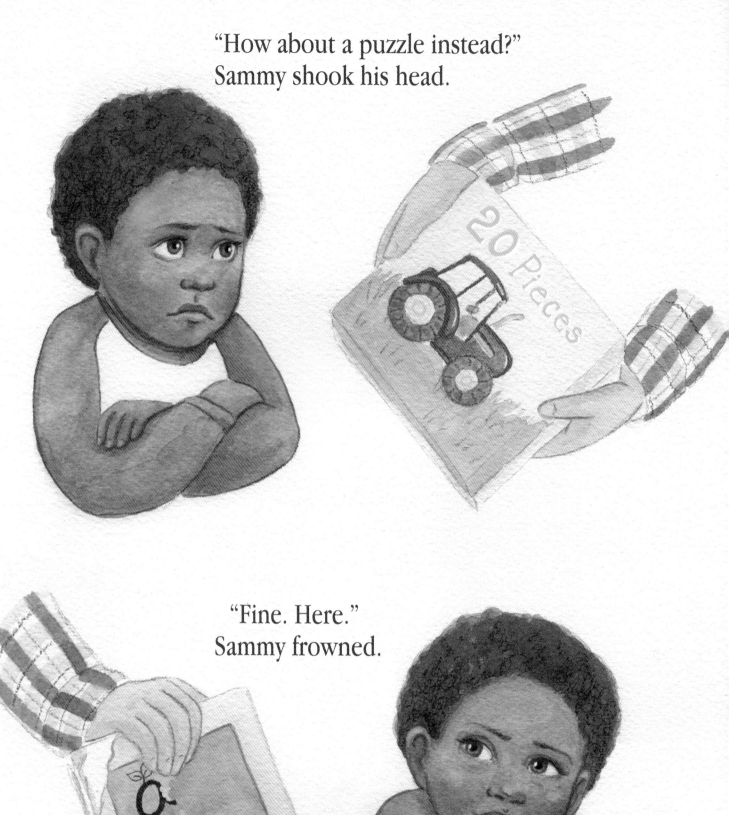

"Fine. Here."
Sammy frowned.

This was hopeless. She should be keeping books away from this little rascal, not offering him new ones.

Libby decided to mind her own business.

"Book! Book!" Sammy reached for her book.

"Nuh-uh." Libby held it out of reach. "This here's my favorite. Pick another."

Sammy looked sadder than a cowboy without a horse.

"Don't give me that sappy-eyed stare," said Libby.

Sammy pointed to her book. "Cowboy."

"You like cowboys too, huh?"

Sammy nodded. "Pease?"

"Oh, all right. But promise to treat it like gold."

Sammy's eyes lit up.
He hugged that book
tighter than a rodeo
rider holds on to a bull.

Hopping horny toads! thought Libby. *What if I've got this all wrong? Maybe my job isn't about protecting books after all. . . .*

"C'mon, Sammy. Want to help me rustle up some readers?"

In two shakes, Libby and Sammy were galloping to the playground with new stacks of Wanted posters.

Slap!

The Wild Reader

Slap!

Read-Aloud Rascal

Critic Kid

Slap!

The kids gathered 'round.

"Hey, that looks like me," said Zoey. "I love animal books!"

"Look at this one. I can read to my little brother like that," said José.

"Book recommendations? I'd be great at that," said Sasha.

"What's all this about?" asked Bryan.

"It's the Library's Most Wanted," said Libby. "The library wants kids to love books, and the job of a deputy—I mean—librarian is to help make that happen."

"So, now what?" asked Sasha.

Libby grinned. "C'mon to the library."

Aunt Nora had given
her a job, and Libby
took it very seriously.

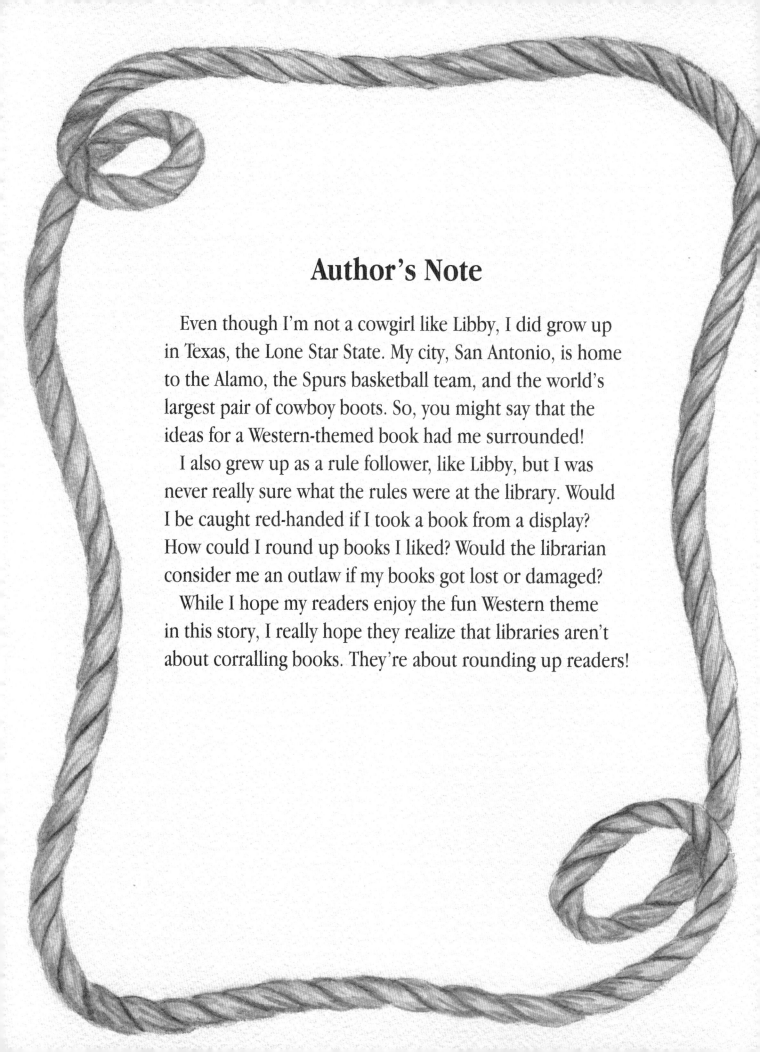

Author's Note

Even though I'm not a cowgirl like Libby, I did grow up in Texas, the Lone Star State. My city, San Antonio, is home to the Alamo, the Spurs basketball team, and the world's largest pair of cowboy boots. So, you might say that the ideas for a Western-themed book had me surrounded!

I also grew up as a rule follower, like Libby, but I was never really sure what the rules were at the library. Would I be caught red-handed if I took a book from a display? How could I round up books I liked? Would the librarian consider me an outlaw if my books got lost or damaged?

While I hope my readers enjoy the fun Western theme in this story, I really hope they realize that libraries aren't about corralling books. They're about rounding up readers!